THE SEETHING BELOW

TERRY CAMPBELL

THE SEETHING BELOW © 2025 Terry Campbell

Published by Graveside Press
graveside-press.com

Editing: Kelley York
Cover illustration: Sleepy Fox Studio
Interior Formatting: Sleepy Fox Studio

Digital 978-1-969655-28-9
Paperback (Trade) 978-1-969655-27-2

No part of this book has been created using Generative AI. Graveside Press and its authors do not consent for our works to be utilized in any form of machine learning training.

GRAVESIDE⚶PRESS

CONTENT NOTES

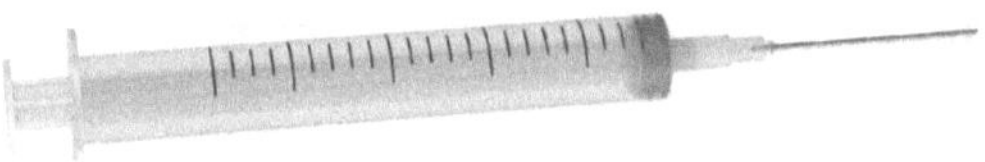

For a list of potentially triggering content,
please skip to page 39.

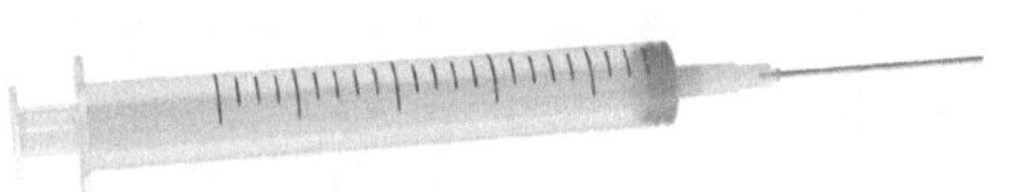

Somewhere near the corner of West and 37th, where drug deals go down with all the conspicuity of a day of bartering at a flea market, and rock cocaine is more plentiful among twelve-year-olds than baseball cards and POG milk caps, a junkie's trembling fingers drop a well-traveled hypo, its corroded length infested with thousands of HIV bugs, to the grimy sidewalk, where it bounces twice, gets kicked a few times, then slides through a vent and into the world below.

Ten blocks away, a child of five blows air into one of several spent condoms he finds scattered along the sidewalk, joyously making a balloon until one slips from his tiny hands and flits through the air, releasing a farting noise that elicits giggles, and lands in a current of run-off from an afternoon shower, where it drifts downstream toward a gutter and into the world below.

On the other end of the city, near a burned-out apartment building where the ghosts of memories past play a grainy theater screen to drug deals gone sour, a rookie cop with a wandering mind accidentally kicks an empty round while investigating a drive-by, sending the metallic shell bouncing through a grate, where it rattles between the grills momentarily before slipping through and dropping into the world below.

In the darkness, three inanimate objects, devoid of life in and of themselves, yet each one having a role in the lives of others in one form or another, come to rest in the bowels of the sewers miles away from each other. Down here, past the bustle of those above, past even the tunnels where the subways cut through at all hours, where the only witnesses are giant sewer rats well-nourished on the filth of the city and the lifeless bones of those who died long ago, these three inanimate objects lift and rise on the viscous current of a substance not quite liquid, not quite solid. The gelatinous ooze rises over them, caresses them, swallows them up, and pulls them forward.

In three different sections of the underworld, three inanimate objects move forward, guided by an unseen force, turning and dipping, mindlessly navigating the twists and turns of the sewer system, one slowly nearing the next until the three trails of deliquescent mire combine and meld at the foot of something not quite living, not quite inanimate, in a place where there are no rats or bones to watch, where there is nothing alive, where the smell of death hangs heavy in what little air infiltrates the stagnant environment.

Shafts of dust-laden light penetrated the broken windows of the venerable old church, falling softly on the rows and rows of worn pews and trodden carpet. Near the altar, a priest sat in the confessional, patiently listening to one of the few inhabitants of the city who bothered to confess their sins. A young man wearing dark, round sunglasses lingered near the great double doors leading into the place of worship. He whipped his shoulder-length dirty brown hair aside and peered back toward the altar. A lone elderly woman sat in the first pew, lost in prayer and oblivious to all. Aware that no one was watching, the young man grabbed a handful of religious leaflets and moved swiftly but quietly out into the city streets.

Once outside, he looked up into the gray sky. Weak sunlight strained to filter through the omnipresent cloud cover. He pushed his sunglasses higher on his nose and examined the leaflets.

The first one read: *Is the end near?*

The young man held the pamphlet high and repeated the words in a shrill cry.

People shuffled by to and fro, lost in their own lives, stuck in the ruts of the roads they traveled, unable to climb out.

"I said, '*Is the end near?*'" the young man repeated.

A derelict digging through a trash can raised his head momentarily, but that was the only attention the young savior got.

"Can you feel it?" the man in the dark sunglasses asked, this time his voice barely a whisper. "Can you *feel* it in the air?" He nodded to himself and looked around. A bead of sweat found its way onto his glasses and trickled down the lens.

Trash blew by on the warm breeze. An odor of filth—an odor that would gag anyone not accustomed to it—drifted through the air. Street people shuffled along; businessmen bustled.

But no one cared.

"Something is coming," the young man said. "And it isn't me."

Clint Ballard picked up the phone on the fourth ring, almost slipping on the wet bathroom floor. As he tilted his head toward the earpiece, water dribbled into his ear canal. He hated that.

"Ballard!" an excited voice shouted from the other end. "What the hell took you so long?"

Mason. His boss at KDFS-Channel 8, the news station where Clint Ballard was employed as a reporter.

"I was in the shower," Clint said, finger twisting in his ear.

"I don't pay you to be clean, Ballard. Besides, you won't be clean long where you're going."

"Come again?"

"I want you to go down to 5th and Union, find this old street lady—" Mason said.

"Wait, wait," Clint interrupted, grabbing a pencil. "Let me write it down."

"There's a fucked up old broad named Maria down there who claims she sees things floating in the air. I want you to check it out."

Clint paused. "You're kidding, right?" He was not ready for this so early in the morning.

"Just do it, Ballard."

"C'mon, Mason. What kind of angle is that?"

"It's a crazy old lady seeing things. Just do it, will ya?" Mason argued.

"Another crazy street person?"

"It's human interest. Just get down there and do it. Take Smitty with you."

"All right," Clint agreed.

"Can I count on you?"

"Yeah, yeah."

"All right. That's what I want to hear. Get back with me."

The other end of the line fell silent. Clint hung up the phone, ran his fingers through his wet hair, and sighed. Another interview with a crazy. He could remember a time when news was interesting, when people gave a damn about what was happening in the world around them.

Oh well, it paid the bills and allowed him to stay in this shit-hole of an apartment. In the long run, he supposed, Clint Ballard didn't give a damn about anything any more than the next guy.

"Hey, Jesus," the passerby taunted. "When you comin' back? Oh, that's right. You're already here, ain't ya?"

The young man in the dark sunglasses turned to face the heckler. "I am here. I walk among you. I wait for the time to take my children back with me to the Divine Kingdom."

The stranger clamped a hand on the young man's shoulder. "You a fuckin' loon, you know that?" He laughed hysterically and made his way through the masses, resuming his plodding through what served as his existence.

The man who called himself Jesus Christ dropped to his knees, returning his attention to the steam grate embedded in the concrete sidewalk. The odors below were even fouler than the stench of the world above. Steam rose through the grill, and with it came an underlying damp coolness that was missing on the streets of the city. It was almost soothing.

Jesus Christ smiled. *Deception is the way of evil*, he thought.

The young man leaned forward and peered into the grate. He could see only a brief reflection in the standing water that collected in the tunnels below. He reached a hand into his jacket pocket, retrieved one of the leaflets he had taken from the church, and folded it double. The young man then dropped the leaflet through the grill, lowering his head so that he could peer into the dark subterranean world. At first, he could see the piece of paper only as a faint glow of white against darkness. As his eyes adjusted, he could discern the leaflet more keenly. He watched it for a moment, ignoring the barbs and insults of the masses as they shuffled past him. The leaflet sat still in the blackness for a long while, and then it moved. Only slightly at first. It made a few herky-jerky movements, then seemed to catch in a stream or breeze. But Jesus Christ knew there was no breeze or stream below. Still, he watched the leaflet move onward as if taken by some unseen hand, and he knew.

"Yes," he mumbled under his breath. "Yes, you know, too. And it's just as I expected. They're all full of shit."

"Well, this should be easy," Smitty said, hoisting the bulky camera over his shoulder. "All we have to do is find one crazy street person in this neighborhood. Piece of cake, huh?"

Clint gave his photographer first a half-grin, then the finger. "I can assure you, Smitty. I'm just as thrilled about this assignment as you are."

"Do we even know this woman's name?"

"Maria," Clint answered. "That's all Mason gave me."

"Well," Smitty said. "I guess we can just start asking around."

They took a moment to lock the van before turning their attention to the desolate surroundings. Trash littered the streets; makeshift sleeping quarters lined the walls of the dilapidated buildings. Condoms and broken liquor bottles and everything else that made Clint thankful for his little shit-hole apartment covered the ground.

"Can you imagine living like this?" Smitty asked.

"I *can* imagine it; don't want to."

The reporter and cameraman approached a trio of scraggly looking men dressed in rags passing a bottle of wine around. The men eyed Clint and Smitty suspiciously, a hint of brightness still lingering in the washed-out, bloodshot eyes.

"Excuse me, gentlemen," Clint began. "Could you tell me where I might find a woman named Maria?"

"How much?" one of the bums asked, a single yellow tooth glowing amid the stubble that surrounded his rancid mouth.

"How much? What do you mean?"

The man rubbed his fingers together.

"Oh," Clint realized. "Five dollars?"

"No," the bum said immediately.

"Five bucks will buy at least three bottles of that cheap poison."

The transients looked at each other, then their leader nodded his head in agreement. Clint dug in his wallet and retrieved a wrinkled five-dollar bill. He started to hand it to the man when it slid from his grip and fell to the vent at his feet. It teetered on a bar for a moment, then dropped into the world below. "Dammit," Clint cursed.

The bum held his hand out again. Clint pulled another fiver from his wallet and handed it to the man. "You'll just go after that one, too. After we're gone."

The man glanced nervously into the grate then looked back at Clint, shaking his head. "Where that money went...I want no part of."

"Now, where's Maria?"

The street person motioned for Clint and Smitty to go around the corner and into the adjacent alley. The two newsmen glanced at each other as if to confirm the other's willingness to travel deeper into the filthy shantytown. But they knew they had no choice.

"Thank you, gentlemen," Clint said to the bums. "Don't drink it all in one place."

Clint turned and headed toward the alley while Smitty shifted the camera and started after him. They waded through sleeping street people and trash before turning into the alley. More lean-tos and homemade cots lined the walls, and Clint wondered if the police ever ventured into this part of town. It wasn't likely. The only people around were the street folks, so who was left to complain? But it wasn't the fault of average cops. Clint was pretty sure the top brass gave little concern to the plight of this area. "Where do we start?"

"I don't know, but we don't have enough five-dollar bills to hand out to every asshole here," Smitty answered.

"Oh, cut them some slack. They're victims of a system that doesn't give half a dozen shits about them. What other choice do they have?"

"Yeah, whatever. Oh, excuse me, ma'am," Smitty called out to a bent-over old woman. "Can you tell me where I might find Maria?"

The lady's round face peered out from the confines of a stained toboggan. Clint was reminded of the shrubbery woman in *Monty Python and the Holy Grail*. "Who wants to know?"

"We're reporters," Clint said. "We'd like to ask Maria a few questions."

"No kidding?" the woman asked incredulously. "What would you want to know from Maria?"

"We were told she sees things moving by themselves," Clint explained.

The old woman chuckled. "Is that what you want Maria for? 'Cause she sees things flyin' through the air?" She cleared her throat; the sound disgusted Clint. "Honey, you don't need Maria. Just ask anyone here, they'll tell ya."

"What do you mean?"

"Hell, stay around long enough, you'll see it yerself," the woman answered.

"You mean you've personally seen these things moving around?" Clint gave a wary glance to his partner, who started the camera rolling. The woman nodded. "What are they? What do you see moving around?"

The woman shrugged. "I don't know. Trash, mostly. Beer bottles, drugs, our beds. Different things."

"And when you say they move, what do you mean exactly?"

"They just move."

"Like because the wind blows them?" Clint asked.

"No, they just *move*. Mostly they fall in the gutter and disappear, but sometimes..." The woman's voice faltered, and she looked around nervously. "Sometimes, the gutter comes for them."

The woman turned and shambled away.

"What do you mean by that? The gutter comes after them?" Clint called after her.

The woman disappeared behind a moth-eaten blanket hanging from a pole.

She did not answer.

"What do you think?" Clint asked Smitty as they rolled down the street in the van.

"I think I wasted half a tape," Smitty replied.

"But what do you think they're seeing?"

"Oh, c'mon, Clint. They're not seeing anything. I don't know. The wind, a street sweeper knocking things around. Who knows?"

Clint peered out the window and watched the filth roll by. "When will it all end?"

"What?" Smitty asked, taking his eyes off the road.

"The filth. The decay. I mean, it can't just keep going, can it? There has to be a stopping point, right? When do you realize this and do something about it?"

"Methinks you think too much," Smitty said. "Hey, how about lunch? After we get out of this side of town, that is."

Clint nodded and continued to stare out the window until something caught his eye. "Stop the van."

"What?"

"Just pull over."

Smitty veered the van to the side of the road and slowed it to a halt.

"What is that?" Clint asked, pointing out the van's passenger-side window.

A long, narrow concrete path pulled away from the side of the road, its plane slowly tapering at an angle so that it ended well below the surface of the main road. Tall brick walls lined either side of the passage, coming to an end at a great wall. Tunnels were cut into this enclosure, offering a view into a dark void.

"That?" Smitty asked. "That's one of the entrances into the sewer system. A big drainage area. Why?"

"Something doesn't look right," Clint said, his eyes studying the scene. "I can't place it, but something is wrong. Don't you see it?"

"No," Smitty said. "I don't. You feeling all right? You get enough sleep last night?"

Clint held his hand up to silence his partner. "I'm fine. It's just that..." He snapped his fingers. "That's it!"

"What's it?"

Before his partner could get an answer, Clint was already out of the van and trotting down the incline toward the tunnels. Smitty sighed and followed.

"What's it?" he asked again when he caught up with Clint. "What are you talking about?"

"Where's the trash?" Clint said, extending his arms to either side. "This place should be filthy. It catches all the runoff from that shantytown, from this whole nasty side of the city. So where's all the trash?"

"It's gone down into the sewer, Clint. It's a drainage system. Water carries the trash into those tunnels."

"No, no," Clint said, looking around. "Not that well. Look around. This place is spotless. You could eat off it. There's no scum on the concrete. No algae in the shade. Nothing. When's the last time you saw a spotless drainage ditch?"

"I don't know, man. Maybe it is a little strange, but I don't see why it's that big a deal."

"What did that old lady say about the gutters coming for the trash?" Clint asked.

"What are you saying?"

"I don't know, Smitty. Oh, nevermind. You're probably right."

When they got back to the van, the mobile phone was ringing. Clint picked it up. It was Mason.

"Have you found the old woman? Well, forget it. Get over to Central Square. The Jesus guy's gone nuts."

The Jesus guy's gone nuts. Was that ever a redundant statement.

Clint knew who Mason meant. In fact, the whole town knew who the "Jesus guy" was: some young kid who had strolled into the city a few years ago claiming to be Jesus Christ. No one knew where he came from; no one knew where he lived now. He just wandered the streets, giving impromptu sermons from time to time and urging people to repent. Clint had interviewed the man once, but the piece had turned into little more than a time killer on the actual news broadcast. The guy couldn't be taken seriously; it was common knowledge he wasn't all there.

But as Clint and Smitty arrived at Central Square, they realized the Jesus guy had really gone off the deep end this time. A large crowd had gathered in Central Square, the city's once glorious financial district. Standing atop a first floor fire escape was Jesus himself.

Clint looked at Smitty. "Better than chasing down bag ladies."

"This could be interesting. I've never seen such a crowd before. Not where Jesus is concerned, anyway," Clint said.

Smitty grabbed the camera and the two men fought their way through the crowd to get a better position. Several rival news crews were already on the scene. Clint looked up through the tangle of boom microphones and wires at the skinny savior on the fire escape. Dressed in a green army fatigue jacket and sporting the omnipresent round sunglasses, the man looked for all the world like John Lennon. Clint couldn't help but grin as the words to "Imagine" began to play in his head. He could tell from his position that Jesus' hands were full, but of what, Clint could not yet discern. Smitty stopped just under the fire escape and positioned the camera's eye upward.

"Friends and loved ones!" Jesus shouted. "What do I hold in my hand?"

Clint squinted to see. The surrounding bustle made it difficult to focus his vision. It looked like Jesus had some type of papers clutched in his fingers.

"I'll tell you what I have! Lies! Pure, unadulterated lies! Lies! Lies! Lies!" he shouted above the din of the crowd. "And you can pick up these lies at any bookstore, any library, any church in the city!"

"What does he have?"

"I can't really tell," Clint answered, then happened to look to the ground. A flash of white caught his eye, and he knelt to retrieve what he had seen. It was a religious flyer, the type available in the lobbies of churches. It was muddy and trampled by the crowd, but Clint could make out the title: "Ten Modern Day Signs of the Return of Jesus Christ". He looked back up at the Lennon look-alike. In his grasp, he held scores of the leaflets. Clint showed the flyer to Smitty.

Smitty grinned. "This is *definitely* more interesting than chasing bag ladies."

"Do you know why these are lies?" Jesus continued. "Do you know why these words lie to you, my children? Is it because I, your Lord and Savior, say so? No! It's because they are of Satan! Satan lives below us! He distributes these lies so that you may be steered in the wrong direction! He forces you to turn away from my Holy truth so that he may corrupt you! And how will he corrupt you?"

"You are rolling, aren't you?" Clint asked Smitty.

"Damn straight."

The crowd buzzed with excitement and anticipation. Jesus really had them worked up. It was as if they were expecting something on a miraculous level, just as the people of Jerusalem once had. And once again, Jesus Christ did not let them down.

"With these!" he shouted, retrieving items from a plastic bag at his feet.

"What does he have?" Clint asked. Smitty shrugged.

"These are the tools of corruption! These are what have turned our fair world into a seething snake pit of filth and unholiness! And we have embraced these tools of evil with all our blackened hearts!"

Clint could just make out what the man had.

It was a bunch of trash. Granted, it was an interesting collection of trash, but it was still just trash. He couldn't get a good look at everything, but he could see syringes, beer cans, Styrofoam cups, newspapers. It looked like Jesus had whacked a street cleaner over the head and stolen his bag. Mason was right: this guy had totally flipped.

"But all this time, we were living it up and just enjoying ourselves like there was no tomorrow, and it was taking its toll on our world, on our city! The more we indulged, the more we enjoyed ourselves! The less we cared about our neighbor! The more we cared about only the self and not the community! And don't think this wasn't going unnoticed. When hate and indifference is allowed to grow unabated over an extended period of time, they can't help but take shape! And that, my friends and loved ones, is what I'm here today to show you!"

With those words, Jesus grabbed the plastic garbage bags stuffed with trash and began dumping their contents over his enrapt audience. Filth, mystery liquids, tainted hypodermics, spent condoms and the like showered down on the screaming crowd, catching on the warm breeze for a moment before falling to the street. The mob stumbled backwards, shaking their heads frantically to free themselves from any falling debris. Even the news crews—Clint and Smitty included—stepped briskly away from the fire escape.

Clint was the first to notice; he hadn't earlier due to the throng of people situated over top of it, but the retreat of the horde had exposed a large sewer grid built into the city street.

Condoms and religious leaflets fluttered gently and came to a stop atop the metal grid. Beer cans and needles bounced and danced before rolling to a standstill. The mob's hysteria at the impromptu shower had diminished, and its attention returned to the Jesus guy.

"I'm here to tell you that the end is near, but not the end predicted in these lie-ridden pamphlets!" Jesus said, launching another batch of the paper missiles. "This...*this* is an end caused by mankind and only mankind! This is our own downfall! Stand back and watch! Stand back and realize our fates!"

Jesus held his hands high, throwing his head back to the monochrome sky. The crowd watched the skies as well, as if expecting a monsoon of biblical proportions to assault the city. But the surprise came from below instead.

Clint felt it in his feet at first. He looked down and noticed that he was still straddling the corner of the vent, and the vibrations of a distant rumble trembled in his toes. Murmurs floated through the crowd as the noise grew louder. The physical shaking intensified as well, and soon, the clanging of the metal grid could be heard. The trash littering the vent began to quiver and dance; isolated pieces fell through the cracks and into the world below.

"Witness the birth of your child, dear people, for you are the ones who bore it!" Jesus cried.

The rumbling intensified; windows of nearby buildings rattled. Mortar dust sifted from the bricks. Clint peered into the grid and could not believe what he was seeing. A thick, grayish, semi-opaque muck was pushing its way up between the metal rods of the grate, ensnaring the pieces of garbage and covering them like a prehistoric insect being fossilized in tree sap. Stunned into silence, the crowd stared in wonder at the thick liquid. Incredibly, the garbage that had landed away from the grid began to skid along the asphalt as if being drawn by a great magnet, becoming enveloped by the ooze.

"Ladies and gentlemen, *that is your end!*" Jesus concluded.

Slowly, the gelatinous substance trickled back into the sewer, taking with it all the trash and refuse that Jesus had showered upon the crowd. When it was completely gone, the sewer framework was sparkling clean.

"Did you get all that?" Clint asked Smitty, his voice full of awe and wonder.

Smitty cleared his throat. "To tell you the truth, I don't know. I think I stopped consciously filming some time back."

"Excuse me," Clint called out to the man in the dark sunglasses. "Mr....uh..."

"You know who I am," the man said, as Clint fully expected him to. "You're just too afraid to say it."

"Of course," Clint said, offering a smile.

Clint took a closer look at the man who had delivered his stirring sermon from the fire escape. He looked a lot smaller and less powerful close up.

"I was wondering if you might answer a few questions. Do you remember me? Clint Ballard? I interviewed you a while back."

"Oh, yes," Jesus said. "And if memory serves me correctly, you presented the interview with a not-so-subtle humorous slant." His dark eyes seemed to burn into Clint's brain.

"Well..." Clint glanced at Smitty. His associate offered no help. "About that. You see... I..."

Jesus held up a hand to silence Clint. "It's completely forgotten, child."

Child? Clint thought. This kid was almost young enough to be his son.

"I don't expect the souls of this day and age to have any more compassion for the Lord's word than did the Romans. At least, I trust I won't be crucified." He grinned, and only then did Clint realize the man was joking. "Now, what do you wish to speak to me about?"

"About tonight," Clint said, as if his answer should be obvious. "About what happened. Well...what *did* happen? I mean, we saw it; we all saw it. But...*what* did we see? Was it Satan? Was it evil?"

Jesus shook his head slowly. "No, not Satan, and not necessarily evil. It is merely life. Just as my father saw fit to begin the stirrings of life with a tiny organism on the ocean floor, so has this creation seen light."

"So, it's God's creation?" Clint asked.

"No, not at all. It is man's."

"Man's?"

"Indeed. We've allowed our greed, our avarice, our apathy to consume us. With each passing day, a little more of our souls die; pieces flake off and fall unseen and unnoticed. We simply turn our backs on it. But though we refuse to see, we can no longer pretend it doesn't exist, for it is here."

"*What* is here?" Clint asked.

Jesus shook his head. "Everything bad about us, about our world, our city has manifested itself; it has found life. It feeds on the physical refuse; it gains its sustenance from such. But it feeds mentally on the qualities that make mankind an inferior animal."

"But what is it?"

"It is our doom," Jesus said. "It has grown unchecked, and soon, it will expand beyond our boundaries. Rest assured, my good man. It is our doom."

A week had passed since the awesome display in Central Square. More and more people were witnessing the cleansing of the streets, the taking of the filth. The city had never looked nicer, never been cleaner. The denizens of the metropolis were beginning to think that whatever was occurring was a *good* thing.

Until people started disappearing.

Clint looked nervously behind him at the rows and rows of seats crammed into the meeting room at the City Hall. The place was full of city officials, police, the mayor, news teams from all the major networks and newspapers, and concerned citizens. Smitty stood near the pulpit working the camera. Up front, the meeting was raging in full-swing.

"We need to call in the National Guard!"

"Declare a state of emergency!"

"Poison the sewer system!"

The appearance of the living organism that had evidently taken up residence far below the city streets was a topic of intense debate. People were dying by the scores now. And folks were terrified. Terrified people demanded answers, but there were none to be found.

"It took my baby!" a woman screamed hysterically. "Just grabbed her and pulled her into the gutter!"

"Children are dying!" a councilman shouted.

"May I say something here?" Clint asked, unable to contain his opinion any longer. "Excuse me! Ladies and gentlemen!"

The din of the crowd finally subsided. "We as a people coexisted with this entity when it was absorbing merely what we didn't want on our streets. Now, when it has decided it wants to take people, we panic." Clint paused a moment, making sure he had the crowd's full attention. "But look at what we have as victims. Transients. Prostitutes. Drug dealers."

"What are you getting at, sir?" the mayor asked.

"At the risk of offending some people, may I say that the creature is still doing the same thing—ridding our streets of what we don't want?"

"It took my baby!" the mother shouted again.

Hoo boy, Clint thought. *Here comes the fun part.* If his theory—or the theory he had adopted from Jesus Christ—was right, then the bloodshot eyes and nervous, paranoid persona of the grieving mother only supported it.

"Please do not misinterpret what I'm about to say. The baby in question was taken from a playground at a nursery school.

There were many small children present, yet it singled out one in particular." Clint looked across the room at the mother. "Ma'am, this is a personal question, but are you addicted to drugs?"

The woman looked shocked. "What the hell's that got to do with anything?"

Clint continued to stare at the woman; the crowd was silent.

"Your child was a crack-baby, wasn't it?"

"This is an outrage!" the mayor shouted. "I fail to see what this has to—"

"Don't you see?" Clint said. "It sensed that. The same way it goes after the needles and the plastic baggies with residue in them, it somehow knew the baby had traces of drugs, had traces of *something* wrong in it."

"Are you saying that this...this thing, will only target the afflicted, the addicted, the...shall I say, *undesirable*," Mason asked his employee.

"Yes, but that's only part of it—a very small part of it. If this thing is that sensitive, if it can detect the faintest hint of the 'imperfect'. Then...then, we're all in trouble. Because none of us are perfect, ladies and gentlemen. This creature goes after everything that's wrong with us. If this is true, then eventually, we'll all become targets. And these victims, they're only symptoms of a bigger disease. The drug users? How many times have rehab and the justice system screwed them over?

Prostitutes? How many of them were forced to the streets by a system that failed them? The transients? How many times have they asked for help with their mental issues and simply fallen through the cracks, just to be shuffled off to whatever parts of the city where people don't have to see them?"

The crowd had gone completely silent.

"And what if this thing gets smarter? What if it learns where the malice truly lies? There would be no stopping it." Clint noticed many members of the council casting nervous glances toward one another.

A murmuring of unsteady voices spread across the hall as the attendants absorbed what Clint was telling them. The mother had fallen to the floor in a fit of either grief or withdrawal. It was impossible to tell which.

"What do we do?" someone in the audience muttered.

"I'll tell you what we can do," a voice said from the back of the room.

Jesus Christ had arrived. *And not a moment too soon,* Clint thought.

The man in the fatigue jacket and Lennon sunglasses ambled through the crowd, taking his time, and moved to the microphone.

"I'll tell you what we have to do," he repeated. "But you have to believe. You have to believe in me; you must believe in yourselves. And most of all, we as a people must come together."

The crowd was massive. People stretched from the police barricade placed in front of the sewer entrance into Central Square and well beyond. Clint had never seen anything like it. The entire city had turned out, just as Jesus Christ had requested. Families were present. Fathers held children tightly. Elderly folks stood alone, staring into the black tunnels of the sewer. People held candles and peered into the night, unsure of what their futures held for them.

"Do you think this will work?" Smitty asked.

"I don't know," Clint answered, scanning the scene. "If what Jesus says is true, then it could be the only answer."

Clint closed his eyes and prayed. He had gotten to know Jesus pretty well over the last few weeks, and he was beginning to believe in what he said.

"Clint, you're not putting too much faith in this guy, are you?"

"I guess we'll know soon enough."

Clint opened his eyes to the sight of cups, hacked spit-wads, and cigarette butts flying through the air unabated by any natural winds. On the ground, broken chunks of liquor bottles and pages from porn magazines skittered along the asphalt, all the refuse meeting up in an unnatural procession headed straight for the blackened maw of the sewer.

Jesus Christ stood on a massive podium placed atop the maintenance walkway that ran above the sewer entrance. There were dozens of microphones in front of his stand, and giant speakers lined the area so that all could hear his words.

"Friends and loved ones, my children, we have gathered here tonight to come together in a show of unity and togetherness in the face of adverse and uncertain times. We have been forced to look ourselves in the eye the past few months, and we've seen what we've refused to see for countless eons."

Clint looked around, studying the gathering. They all seemed to be hinging on every word Jesus said. The guy had charisma; that much was certain.

"We as a people have gotten away from what the Lord's word had intended. And it's not just your generation. It began long ago."

At that point, there was a scream as a young woman pointed at the drainage valley below the walkway where Jesus stood. The slime was coming up from the sewer. Clint pushed his way through the throngs to get a better look, even as most people were inching backward. The gray slime bubbled and popped, slowly climbing forth from the tunnels like the trail of some giant slug.

"Do not be frightened by its presence," Jesus continued to wail. "It is frightened by our show of support. It seeks to frighten us in turn."

There was a loud, blood-chilling scream as the ooze wrapped around the leg of a police officer and pulled him into the main body. The slime crept ever closer over his person until it reached his face. Clint watched in disgust as it burned into the man's skin, melting his features into a viscous goo of red and gray.

Was he a corrupt cop? Did he sell drugs on the side, or take a cut from dealers he busted? Did he let the sex-workers go if they gave him a ride on the side? Or was he just a victim, as any of them could be? Clint didn't want to think about that.

"Only through our show of solidarity will it back down!" Jesus shouted through the microphones. "We must all come together! We must put aside our differences, we must lay down our vices, our traits that brought rise to this vile and wicked beast! Love one another! Love one and all! Sing unto the Lord, for His power is glory!"

The crowd was silenced as they watched the fallen officer, now nothing more than reddened bones jutting from a tattered blue uniform, sink into the gray jelly. Then, it happened.

The first words of John Lennon's "Give Peace a Chance" began to ring out from somewhere deep in the crowd. A few people picked up on the words and began singing about bagism, fagism, thisism thatism. Jesus held his hands high, swinging them about as if directing a massive choir. Candles flickered in the almost nonexistent breeze, people swayed arm in arm, and by the first chorus, everyone was begging that peace be given a chance.

Clint stared over the crowd in awe, a tear welling in his eye. He looked back into the drain, where there remained only a slimy trail of leftover ooze where the creature had been, the asphalt beneath it spotless. It was retreating.

Clint hopped up on a streetlight and shouted, "Louder! Louder!" He waved his free arm while gripping the post with the other and sang along with the crowd, off-key but heartfelt.

Clint had attended concerts before during which the crowd sang along with the tunes, sometimes without the band. But nothing had ever sounded as impressive, as wonderful as this. The entire city had shown up in a last-minute effort to defeat whatever had risen from their evils, and now, the entire city had joined together in an assault as simple as a song.

Then another scream rang through the air. Clint looked back in time to see a hand disappear into the ooze. The crowd, oblivious to the attack, continued to sing. Clint hopped from the lamppost and pushed through the crowd toward the drainage valley. The trail he had seen earlier was gone. The creature was moving forward once again.

"No," Clint muttered. "No."

He looked about in a panic, trying to gain a higher vantage point. He spotted a city bus parked along a curb and ran to it, grabbed the ladder attached to the rear, and climbed on top. From the top, Clint could look over the entire crowd.

He was saddened, heartbroken, and terrified by what he saw.

People were laughing and singing and passing around whiskey bottles and marijuana cigarettes. Kids pushed and frolicked. Couples kissed and fondled one another. Farther away, in the shadows, a drug deal was going down. In the back seat of a police cruiser, a woman was performing fellatio on a man in uniform.

Despite all their efforts, despite the imperative need to work together, people were slowly but surely reverting back to their selves. The gathering had deteriorated into a giant party. Life had returned to normal on the city streets.

"NO!" Clint shouted as loud as he could, but he could still not be heard over the din of the singing. "No, you're fucking up! You're *fucking it all up!*"

Jesus Christ sensed it too; he gripped the handrail of the walkway and shouted toward the crowd.

The rumbling was subtle at first, but then Clint felt the bus moving, slowly rocking back and forth as the noise intensified. Clint dropped to his knees. "Oh, Jesus," he mumbled.

At that moment, a fissure ripped across the middle of Central Square, and the slime bubbled forth like molten lava. Immediately, the sticky semi-liquid ensnared hundreds of people. The bridge that ran across the sewer tunnels began to collapse, and the rail holding Jesus tilted greatly to one side just a moment before the rear of the bus slid into another giant crater. Clint leapt from the bus, grabbed a side-view mirror, and dropped to the hood of a car, wrenching his shoulder in the process.

He watched in horror as the crowd stampeded in full panic like cattle in an electrical storm, the larger, more powerful bovines knocking the weaker to the ground, where they became easy prey to the rapidly expanding entity. The flight factor overpowered Clint's mind, and he leapt from car-top to car-top in a hasty retreat. He passed the van he and Smitty had arrived in, and for a moment, wondered about his partner. The concern didn't last long. Much of the horde had reached what appeared to be a safe point beyond the wide open crevices in the street, but many of them did not stop running then.

But they did stop when they heard the deafening, low growl that emanated from the sewer.

Clint turned back, expecting to see the earth opening once again, unprepared for what he might see.

The ooze had risen into the air, towering high above the fourth floor windows of the surrounding skyscrapers. Even from this distance, the garbage and refuse of a crumbling society that made up the physical components of this amazing new lifeform could be seen. The silhouette continued to shift and change, taking on a vaguely humanoid shape. Somewhere around its head, Clint thought he could make out the glint of intelligence in what could've been the creature's eyes.

"My god. How can we ever stop that?" someone next to Clint said.

It was Smitty. Clint was only somewhat happy to see him. It seemed a moot point now.

"I don't know, old buddy," Clint said. "I just don't know."

The crowd grew eerily quiet as the thing continued to shift and grow. There was a sickening suction sound as the physical pieces in the ooze slipped and changed position, causing air pockets to form and burst. It expanded as it stood before them. More pieces of garbage flew into the substance, and trailers of slime sent forth from the mother body came back with prized additions to the aberration.

"Look!" someone shouted.

All eyes turned to the tiny figure at the foot of the terrifying creature.

It was Jesus Christ.

"Oh my God," Clint whispered. "What's he doing?"

"He's going to meet his maker," someone replied.

"Yes, though I walk in the valley of your shadow," Jesus cried out as he approached the beast. "Yes, I will fear no evil."

"Holy Jesus," Smitty said.

"Yes, holy Jesus," the man next to him said. "Pray for him now."

"Yes," Clint said, his eyes beaming. "He can do it. He's the only one who's known through this whole ordeal. He knew what it was from the start."

"He's gonna get his crazy ass killed," Smitty said.

"No," Clint answered. "He can do it."

"Are you crazy? The guy's a fucking lunatic. He's the epitome of everything that's wrong with this fucked up city. He's the offspring of this environment. He can't beat that thing. He's not God. He's not Jesus. He's just a crazy homeless guy. Nothing could represent everything that's wrong with society better than him."

"No," Clint repeated, his voice barely a whisper in the anxious silence. "No one believes more than him. He believes with one hundred percent of his heart that he is Jesus Christ. Right now, he's the closest thing to a savior we have."

The tiny silhouette of Jesus Christ looked up into the swirling mass of mankind's decay and held his arms wide. He gripped something in one hand.

"What's that?"

"A Bible," Clint said. "It's a Bible."

Jesus Christ threw the book high into the air, striking the creature where its throat might've been. The Holy Book bounced off and flitted to the ground. The creature wanted no part of it.

Another massive guttural rumble emanated from the being. Its slimy, trash-ridden head hovered a moment directly over Jesus, then a black void opened on its surface and the ooze collapsed downward on the small man. The crowd turned away as the screams of their onetime savior echoed through the streets. Something that could've been the dark sunglasses fell to the ground.

"So much for our savior," Smitty said.

But then something happened. Along with the sunglasses, something else dropped, bouncing to the asphalt. A rustle of paper flitted through the air. The sound of breaking glass rang through the night. A clink here. A crash there. Hypodermics crashed to the ground. Religious leaflets took to the sky on the night breeze. One by one, pieces of the creature began to drop away, until suddenly, garbage was crashing all over and falling back into the drainage system. The ooze began to lose its substance, and the streets grew wet with the liquid it left behind. Streams of water raced along the curbs, carrying condoms and bits of trash along with them like runoff from a summer shower. The trails of water joined up at the massive sewer drainage ditch, creating a giant cascade of water that picked up the garbage and swept it into the black tunnels below.

It took a while for the remaining crowd to realize the creature was gone.

Three months had passed since the city had come together on that fateful evening to fight for their lives in a final showdown with their dark side. The streets, immaculate for a week or two, had slowly returned to their old, dismal, trash-strewn selves. What was left of the huge pile of refuse that had been the creature from the sewers was collected and placed in a giant landfill. Clint often wondered: did that do any good? Just pick it up and put it somewhere else? Was that any better?

Clint peered into the bookstore window at the newly published book that portrayed the life and times of Jesus Christ, the man who had saved the city. Someone had no doubt made up a bunch of shit, maybe pieced together an interview here and there, possibly Clint's own, and claimed to have known the man personally—a man who had been virtually ignored before the appearance of the creature.

The sound of a man groaning diverted Clint's attention from the window. He turned to see a foul-looking man openly shooting heroin in the middle of the city in broad daylight.

"Aaah," the man snorted, then noticed Clint's accusing stare. "Good shit."

"You know," Clint said, "Jesus Christ died for our sins."

"More power to him," the junkie said, dropping the syringe on the sidewalk. He gave Clint a rotten-toothed grin and staggered down the street.

Clint watched him until he disappeared into the crowd of people coming and going, caught in the hustle and bustle of their own private hells. He glanced back at the face of Jesus Christ staring out from the book.

Clint retrieved a tissue from his coat pocket, picked up the hypodermic, and tossed it into the trash can.

ABOUT THE AUTHOR

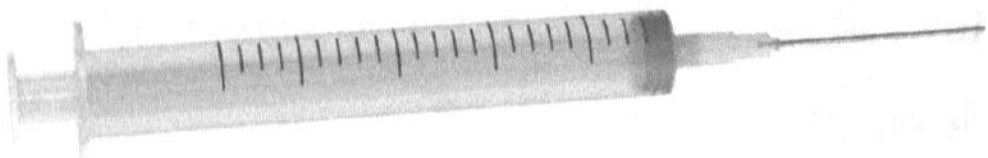

Terry Campbell enjoys writing cosmic horror, folk horror, western horror...and sometimes, just plain horror.

alittlewestofweird.com

CONTENT WARNINGS

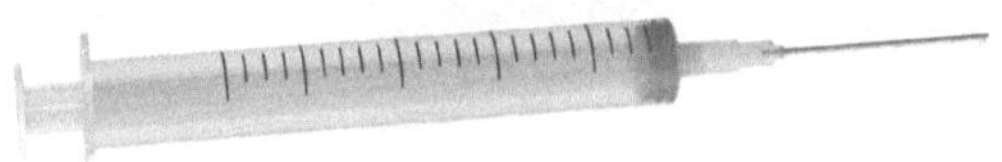

Standard warnings for horror tropes (violence, death, murder) apply to all Graveside Press books. Other potential warnings may include:

- religious themes

- death of children

- substance abuse

- mentions of corrupt law enforcement, including coercion of sex-workers by police

- demeaning language and attitudes of society toward the unhoused, low-income, sex-workers, the mentally ill, and those with addiction issues.

Thank you for supporting Graveside Press and our authors. One of the biggest ways you can help is to leave a star rating or a review wherever you purchased your copy!

STAY SPOOKY.

Want merch, membership benefits, and discounts on
Graveside books?
gsp-shop.fourthwall.com

Wanna come hang out with the ghouls?
gravesidepress.carrd.co